PETER & THE WOLF

SERGEI PROKOFIEV

KVĚTA PACOVSKÁ

minedition

One morning, Peter opened the gate and went out into the big green meadow.

Up in the branches of a tall tree sat the little bird, Peter's friend.

'How quiet it is!' chirped the bird cheerfully.

Then a duck waddled into the meadow. She was pleased
Peter had left the gate open and hurried over to have
a swim in the cool, deep pond.

The little bird saw the duck and flew down
beside it on the grass.
'Tell me, what sort of bird are you, if you can't fly?'

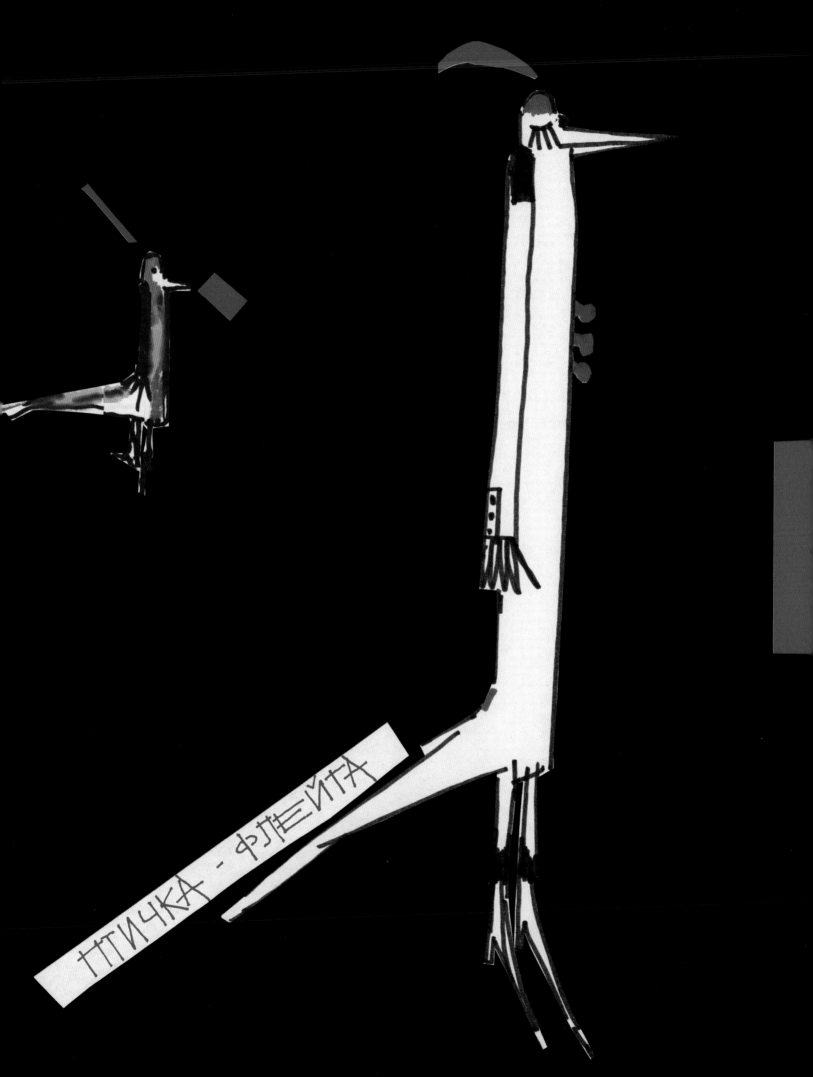

ПТИЧКА - ФЛЕЙТА

The duck quacked 'What kind of bird are you,
if you can't swim?' before diving noisily into the pond.

And the argument went on in this way,
the duck swimming on the pond,
the little bird hopping along the edge of the water.

Suddenly, Peter saw something.
A cat – crawling silently through the grass!

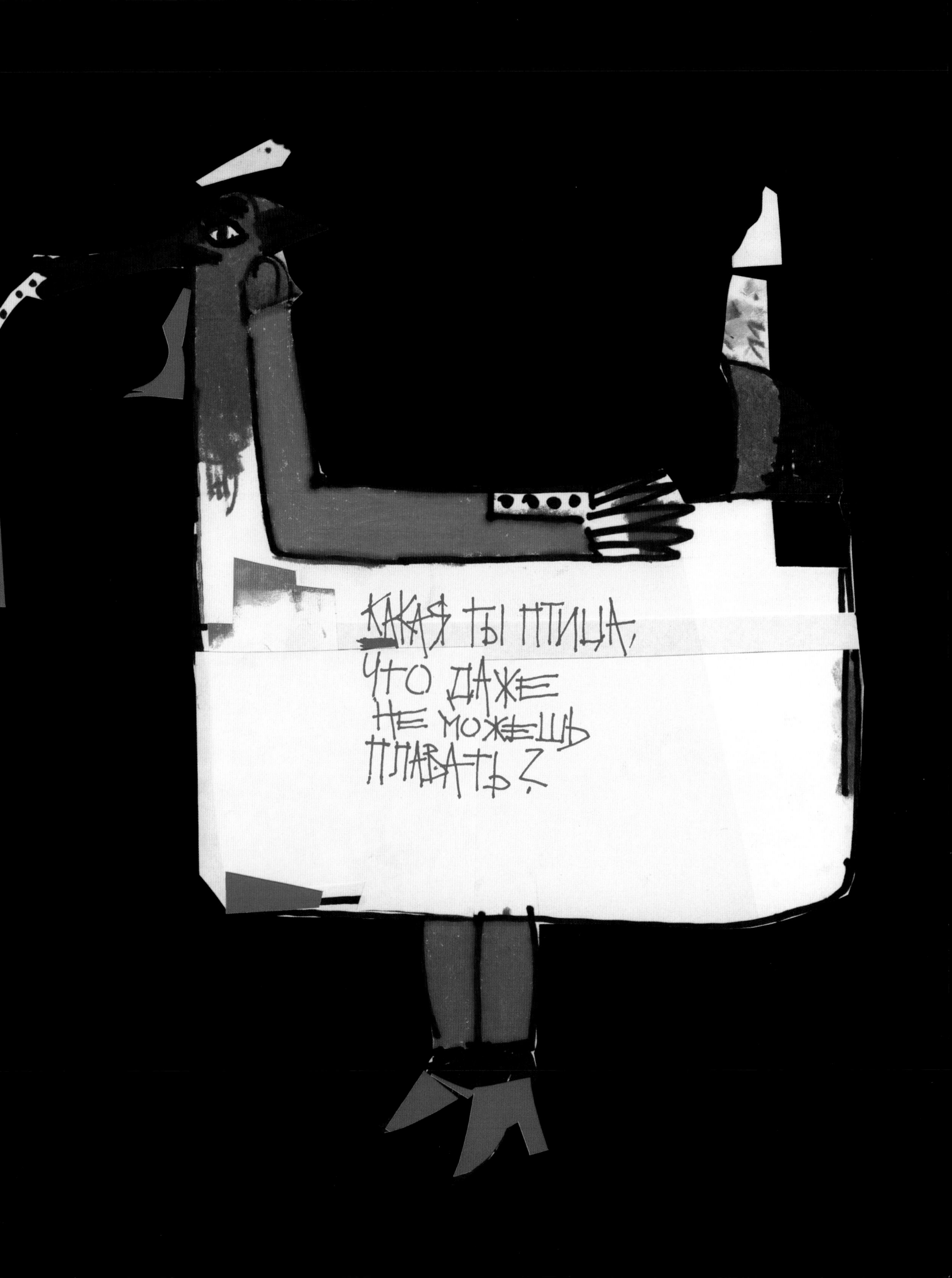
КАКАЯ ТЫ ПТИЦА,
ЧТО ДАЖЕ
НЕ МОЖЕШЬ
ПЛАВАТЬ?

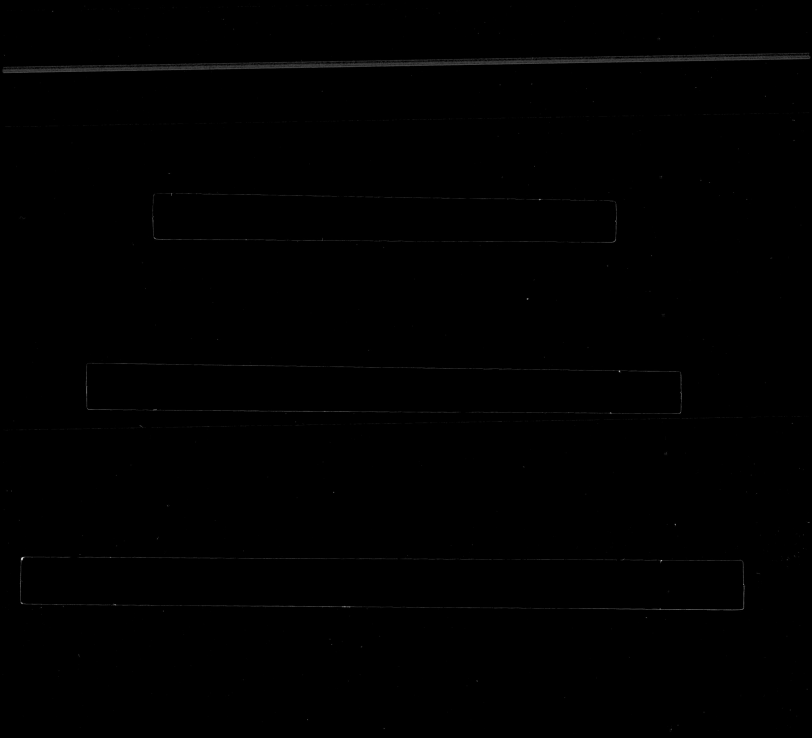

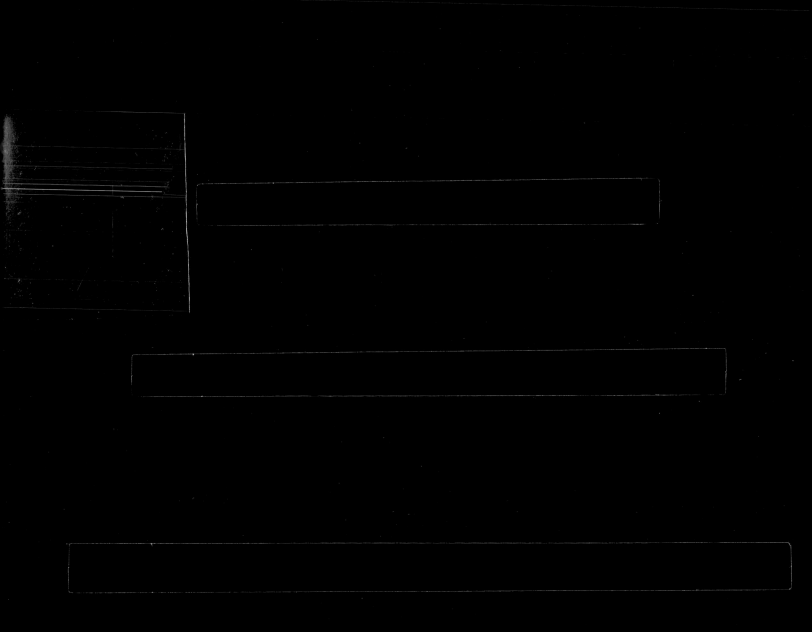

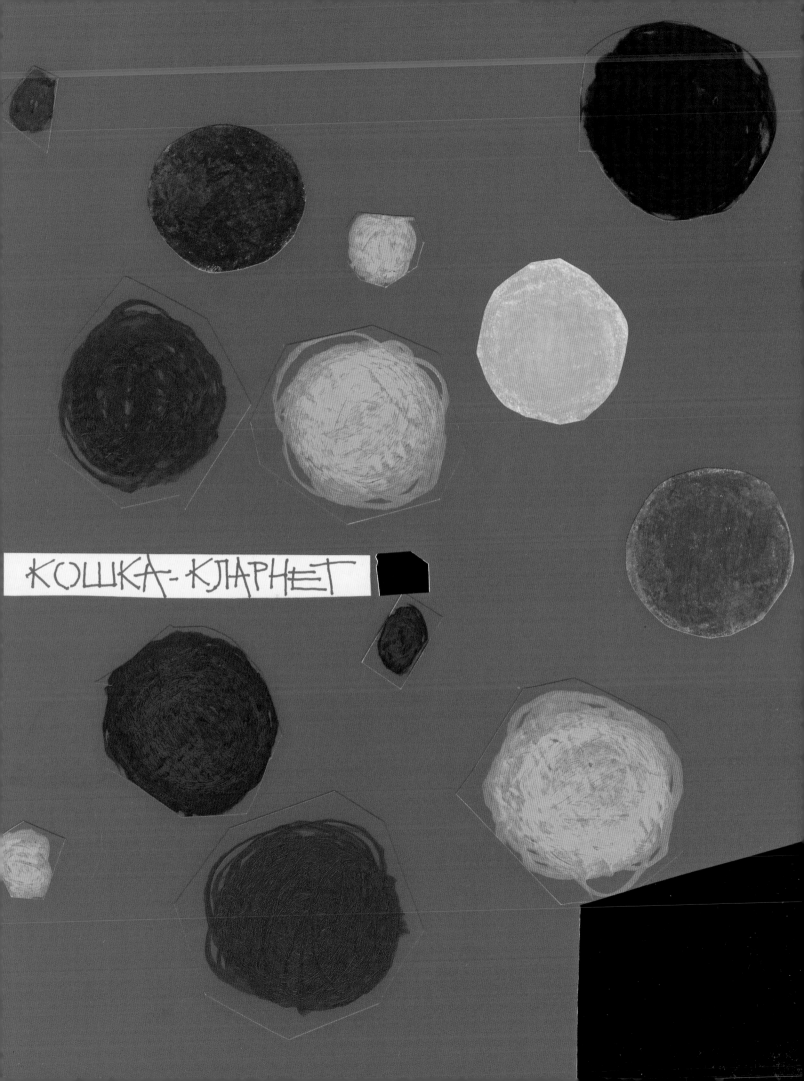

КОШКА-КЛАРНЕТ

The cat thought:
'While the bird is busy arguing, I'll grab her!'

Stealthily, she crept forwards.

'Look out!' called Peter and at once the little bird
flew back up into the tree.
From the middle of the pond,
the duck quacked angrily at the cat.
The cat padded around the tree thinking,
'Is it worth me climbing up there?

КОШКА - КЛАРНЕТ

By the time I get to the top, the bird will have flown away.'

КОШКА-КЛАРНЕТ

Peter's grandfather came out into the meadow.

He was angry with Peter for being there. 'The meadow is a dangerous place! If the wolf comes down from the forest, what will you do?'

Peter was not listening. Boys like him are not
worried about wolves. But Grandfather took
Peter's hand and took him back home,
locking the gate behind them.

As soon as they had gone, a big grey wolf
came down from the forest.
In a flash, the cat jumped up into the tree.
The duck quacked with fright, and not thinking clearly,
flapped out of the pond and on to the grass.

ВОЛК - ВАЛТОРНЫ

She waddled off as fast as she could,

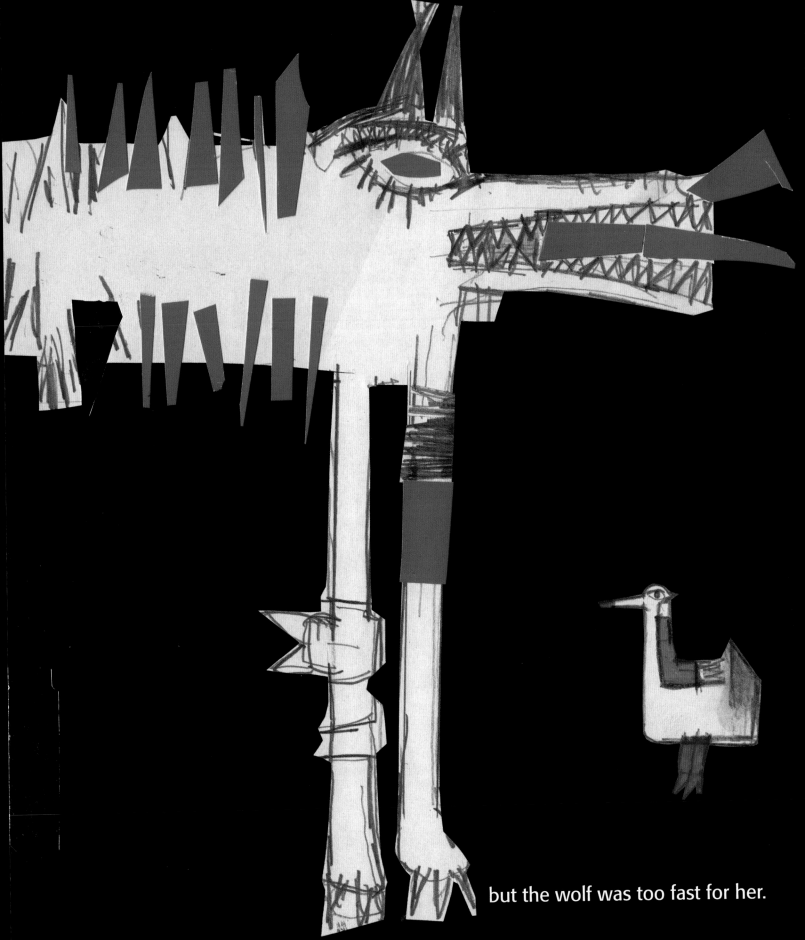

but the wolf was too fast for her.

Gulp! With one swallow he had eaten her up!

So now, this was how things were.

The cat sat on one branch, the little bird on another, not too close to the cat. And the wolf walked round and round the tree, looking up at them with hungry eyes.
Meanwhile, Peter, who was not at all scared, watched from behind the gate.
Quickly, he ran home, found a strong rope and climbed up the high stone wall.

One of the tree's branches hung above the wall and Peter grabbed it, climbing quietly up into the tree.

Peter whispered to the little bird, 'Fly around the wolf's head, but make sure he can't catch you!'

The bird did as she was told, so close to the wolf's head that he snapped angrily at her as she flew past.

The wolf could not bear it. He was desperate to catch the bird, but she was just too quick for him.

While this was going on, Peter made a lasso and carefully lowered it down until it was over the wolf's long grey tail.
Then he pulled the rope with all his might!

At once, the wolf began to twist and pull, trying to get free.

But Peter had tied the other end of the rope to the tree, and the twisting and pulling only made the rope tighter around his tail.

Just then, the hunters came out of the wood, following the wolf's trail, guns ready to shoot.

Peter shouted from the tree, 'Stop! Don't shoot! Little bird and I have caught the wolf. Let's take him to the zoo.'

And so, can you imagine the wonderful sight?

Peter at the front, then the hunters leading the wolf and Grandfather and the cat at the back.

Grandfather shook his head wearily, 'Yes, but what if Peter hadn't caught the wolf? What would have happened then?'

Little bird flew above them, singing happily:
'Hooray for us! Peter and I caught the wolf!'

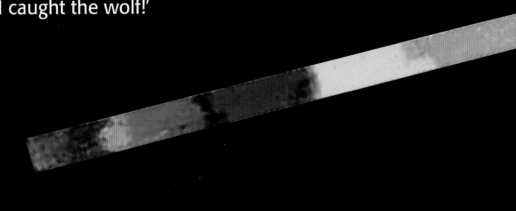

And if you listen very carefully, you can hear the duck quacking in the wolf's tummy, because he had swallowed her whole!

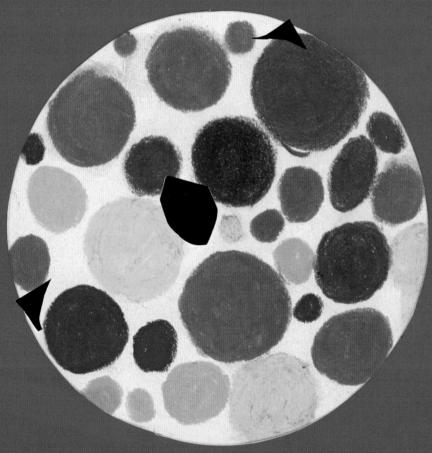

ОХОТНИКИ - БАРАБАНЫ